The world awaits
the gifts that
you alone have come
to give.

With love,

Gina Otto

*

This book is lovingly dedicated
to all Angels everywhere,
who help to give a voice
to those who don't have one ...

Changing the World One Bright Light at a Time.

—Gina Otto

In memory of my beloved sister, Heidi.

—Trudy Joost

Cassandra's Angel

written by Gina Otto
illustrated by Trudy Joost

STERLING CHILDREN'S BOOKS
New York

Cassandra, Cassandra was strolling along.
Cassandra was singing a sing-along song.
She ran through the house and into the hall.
She was going to grab her red rubber ball…
when her mother's voice rang, as some mothers' do,
"Cassandra, come here. I must speak with you."

"Cassandra, Cassandra, your room is a mess.
Your toys are all over. There's jam on your dress.
Cassandra, whatever's the matter with you?
You've turned your whole bedroom into a zoo.
I see lions and monkeys, some birds, and a bear.
There's no neatness at all, not anywhere.
Cassandra, Cassandra, what am I to do?
You're a messy little girl. Just look at you."

Cassandra stopped playing and looked all around.
All she saw was her zoo—no mess to be found.
But mother was right, so it had to be true.
She just wasn't sure what she should do.

I guess I'm a mess, was Cassandra's next thought.
But she did not like that story. NO, SHE DID NOT.

She changed her jam-dress and cleaned up her zoo.
She sang as she worked and danced a bit, too.
All of her toys were put neatly away.
There would be no more messes in her room that day.

She took her red ball and went out to the yard.
That's where she saw Francine, Ken, and Bernard.
"Do you want to play ball?" asked Cassandra with glee.
"Do you want to come over and play with me?"

"Why," they replied, "would we play ball with you?
Your hair is too brown and your eyes are too blue.
Your clothes are too plain, and it wouldn't be fun.
You see, we don't play with just anyone.
You like your dog, Jack. We prefer our cat, Gus.
You're just too different to play ball with us."

Could what they just said really be true?
My hair is different, and my eyes are too.
They don't like my clothes, and they don't like my dog.
So what would they think of my little pet frog?

I guess I'm too different, was Cassandra's next thought.
But she did not like that story. NO, SHE DID NOT.

In class, the students were all asked to paint.
"Here is your paper," said Mr. McQuaint.
"Your task is to paint a small house and a tree,
with seven red flowers and one yellow bee."

Cassandra didn't always remember each rule,
but she was determined to do well in school.
And boy, oh boy, did she love to paint.
How proud she was going to make Mr. McQuaint.

Cassandra took a big brush and let go a sigh.
She closed her eyes tightly then reached way up high.
She started to paint a magnificent tree.
It took all the room—none was left for the bee.

Then all of a sudden, her tree started growing,
faster and faster, not stopping or slowing.
It spread from her easel to Mac's, then to Joe's,
and soon it took over the next seven rows.
With branches on Tom's pad and big leaves on Kate's,
this tree had oranges, pears, apples, and dates.

Her tree was so big it kept growing and soon
its branches reached all the way up to the moon!
This tree was the grandest you could ever find,
and to think it all came from one little girl's mind.

Cassandra was painting a star at the top . . .

When Mr. McQuaint shouted, "Stop it now! STOP!
Cassandra, I'm giving your parents a call.
Now clean up this mess and go sit in the hall."

She picked up the branches and leaves in a flash,
and there was her tree stacked up high in the trash.

I've done it again, she thought very sadly.
I didn't mean to behave so badly.
The truth is I really don't know what I did.
I'm just doing my best at being a kid.
But no matter what, they just don't seem to see.
Then she sighed, *It was such a wonderful tree.*

Soon Mr. McQuaint came out into the hall
with his face much more red than her red rubber ball.

"Cassandra, Cassandra, you're incorrigible. It's true.
What if all of the children began acting like you?"

That great big word made Cassandra feel sad.
She didn't know what it meant. But it had to be bad.
Mr. McQuaint must be right about me.
But I really don't know yet just how I should be.
I guess I'm incorrigible, was Cassandra's next thought.
But she did not like that story. NO, SHE DID NOT.

On her way home she passed through Town Square.
Everyone acted like she was not there.
There must be someone to talk to or call.
She turned the corner and saw City Hall.

"I'll talk to the Mayor," she said with a grin.
So she marched up the stairs and then let herself in.

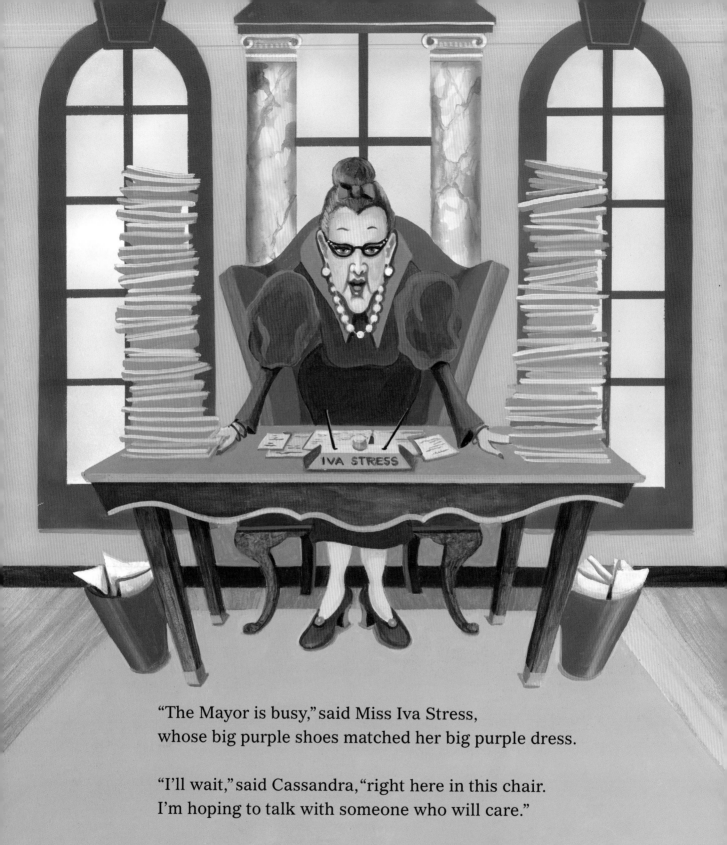

"The Mayor is busy," said Miss Iva Stress,
whose big purple shoes matched her big purple dress.

"I'll wait," said Cassandra, "right here in this chair.
I'm hoping to talk with someone who will care."

Then out walked a very small man through the door,
with fists full of papers and shouting for more.

"Excuse me, Sir Mayor," she said, "if you're free.
I think it is you that I've come here to see.
My mother says that my whole room is a zoo.
She just shakes her head wondering what she should do.
I saw some children and asked them to play,
but they said mean things and then ran away.
Today at my school, when I painted a tree,
I got paint on the classroom and all over me!
The tree that I made kept on growing and soon
its branches reached all the way up to the moon.
So now they are all very angry with me.
I need someone's help, Mr. Mayor, you see."

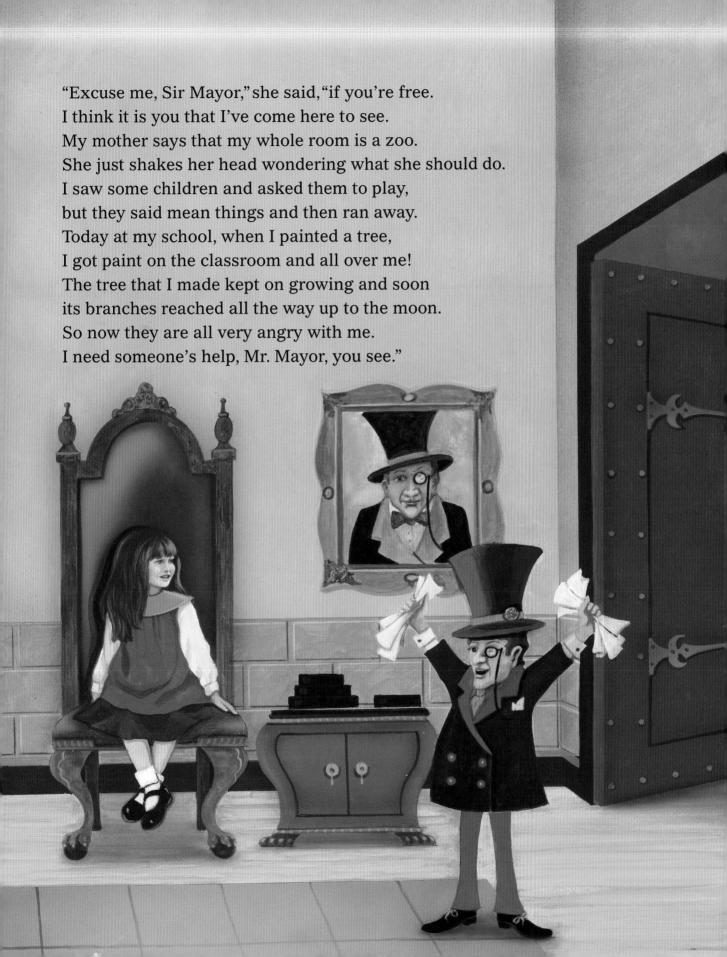

The Mayor stopped short on his way to the door
and dropped all his papers right there on the floor.
"What's all this nonsense about trees and a zoo?
I haven't got time to be talking with you.
I have papers to sign, about seventy-four,
and when that's all done, I've got ninety-two more.
I have so much work. There is no time, I fear.
Now go home, little girl. You are not allowed here."

And before Cassandra could say any more,
Miss Iva Stress whisked her right out the door.

"He was my last hope," said Cassandra out loud.
But nobody heard in that very big crowd.
I feel so alone, was Cassandra's next thought.
But she did not like that story. NO, SHE DID NOT.

She started to run very fast, almost flying.
Cassandra hoped no one would see she was crying.
She soon found herself on the path by the lake.

It just isn't fair. I am one big mistake.
I am a mess. I'm a problem, you see.
I'm incorrigible, and they have no time for me.
Everyone believes it, which must make it true.
Even I start to believe it. Well, I almost do.
But deep down inside I know that I'm good,
though most of the time I feel misunderstood.
I promise myself that I'll work through this test.
I'll try very hard, and I'll do my best.

She climbed a big rock that was standing quite near
and then wiped away her very last tear.
She sat for a while on the rock all alone.
Then Cassandra stood, and she chose to go home.

Somehow I will show them. Somehow they will see . . .
Then she turned and saw her magnificent tree.

And under her tree, sitting there on the ground . . .

was a beautiful Angel,
with wings and a crown.
"Who are you?" she asked,
and again, "Who are you?"

The answer came softly,
Your Angel, that's who.

I've been with you, Cassandra, right here all along.
I felt your sadness and I heard your song.
So I've brought a great secret to give you today.
Come sit here beside me, Cassandra, please stay.
All of those things people have said to you—
They are stories, Cassandra—not one of them true.
You are never just what they believe you to be.
You are even more than you think that you see.
There's a much greater truth. When you look you will find,
the key is right there in your heart and your mind.
It's not what you do. It's about who you are,
for you are as bright as the sky's brightest star.

All of those people who tell stories to you,
they each have the truth deep inside of them, too.
They just have forgotten it over the years,
so now what you hear is their sadness and fears.
It isn't their fault, all those stories they tell.
They believed the stories they were given as well.
Those old kinds of stories create guilt and fear.
But today, Cassandra, those old stories stop here.

You can love people more, for you know what is true.
You now have a choice. It is all up to you.
So shine brightly, Cassandra, to help light the way . . .
and that is the secret I bring you today.

With a soft gust of wind,
the Angel was gone,
and Cassandra could feel
in her heart a new song . . .

I am Cassandra, a bright light, was her very next thought.
And no one could change *that* story. NO, THEY COULD NOT!

STERLING CHILDREN'S BOOKS
New York

An Imprint of Sterling Publishing
387 Park Avenue South
New York, NY 10016

STERLING CHILDREN'S BOOKS and the distinctive Sterling Children's Books logo
are trademarks of Sterling Publishing Co., Inc.

Text & Illustrations © 2001 by Gina Otto

ISBN 978-1-4027-8743-0

Library of Congress Cataloging-in-Publication Data

Otto, Gina,
 Cassandra's angel / written by Gina Otto ; illustrated by Trudy Joost.
   p. cm.
 Summary: When she listens to the people around her, Cassandra feels that she cannot do anything right, but then
a meeting with her Angel gives her a new perspective on herself and others.
 ISBN 978-1-4027-8743-0
 [1. Stories in rhyme. 2. Identity--Fiction. 3. Self-esteem--Fiction. 4. Interpersonal relations--Fiction. 5. Angels--
Fiction.] I. Joost, Trudy, ill. II. Title.
 PZ8.3.O845Cas 2011
 [E]--dc22

              2011009512

Distributed in Canada by Sterling Publishing
 ᶜ/o Canadian Manda Group, 165 Dufferin Street
    Toronto, Ontario, Canada M6K 3H6
Distributed in the United Kingdom by GMC Distribution Services
Castle Place, 166 High Street, Lewes, East Sussex, England BN7 1XU
Distributed in Australia by Capricorn Link (Australia) Pty. Ltd.
     P.O. Box 704, Windsor, NSW 2756, Australia

For information about custom editions, special sales, and premium and corporate purchases,
please contact Sterling Special Sales at 800-805-5489 or specialsales@sterlingpublishing.com.

Manufactured in the United States of America
Lot #:
4 6 8 10 9 7 5 3
10/11

www.sterlingpublishing.com/kids

SPECIAL THANKS to Joni Albers, Errol Ansalone, Lisa Arrabit, Janette Barber, Robert A. Barton, Richard Baskin, Barbara Bridges, Hal Brody, The Colorado Barnes & Noble Angels, Caitlin Corenblith, Joyce DeAndrea, Madalena and Elena DeAndrea, Richard Ellis, Melissa Etheridge, Cheryl and John Evans, Ramiro Fauve, Lynnette Durant Fields, Deborah Forman, Doug Freeman, Emily Freeman, Annette Frehling, Jill Fruktin, Dr. Michael Galitzer, Val Gillen, Leanne Gluck, Steve Hassenberg, Amanda Hawkins, Suzanne Hoyt, Illumination Arts, Gerhard and Virginia Joost, Lee and Irv Kagan, Heidi Krupp and the Krupp Kommunications Team, Robin and Stephen Larsen, Darren Lisiten, Sharon Lee, C.S. Lewis, Jaclyn Libowitz, Deborah Lindholm, Megan Longenbaugh, Ann Lovell, Cindy Magnus, Rosie Magnuson, Joanne Malisani, Ivan and Karen Menchell, Mark Merriman, Coy Middlebrook, Susan Miller, Suzanne Nason, Paul Orfalea, Michael Ortmeier, Meredith Paige, Deb and Chuck Pair, Rob Parke, Al Poppy, Andy Prozes, Laura Heery Prozes, Kevin and Rya Prozes, Susan Ray, Avis Richards and Birds Nest Productions, Jasmine Robinson, Rosie O., Sharon Saks-Soboil, Deb Sandella, Greg Shaw, Matt Sinclair, Susan Smith-Jones, Michele Tamme, Dave Taub and the R2i Team, Cody Teets, David Thalberg, Ted and Barbara Weitz, Marianne Williamson, Lisa Winston Shaw, Jo Ann Wood.

And very special thanks to Marcus Leaver and Sterling Publishing.

ChangeMyWorldNow

Cassandra's Angel is about dropping the
old stories and finding your bright light. Just like
Cassandra did, once we find our bright light
we can shine for the world.

Come visit ChangeMyWorldNow.com and learn how to
create your own personalized page, discover more about what
is going on in our world, connect with others focused on making
the world a better place, and find out how to make a difference.

ChangeMyWorldNow.com is a fun, exciting, interactive
website where you will find a place to belong and
know that your voice is heard.

I look forward to Changing the World with You!

—Gina Otto

CLICK TO CONNECT
or visit
www.ChangeMyWorldNow.com